Volume 1

JUST LIVING

Meditations for Engaging our Life and Times

KENYATTA R. GILBERT

Just Living: Meditations for Engaging Our Life and Times, Volume 1

Dr. Kenyatta Gilbert

CONTENTS

Acknowledgments

For Allison, my love.

PREFACE

I have wanted to write a book like this one for some time now. My first reading of Howard Thurman's timeless treasure *Meditations of the Heart* nearly two decades ago caused the catalyzing stir. Whether prepping with it before facilitating a group discussion with seminarians in my spiritual formation course or sitting alone days on end gathering jewels of insights from his take on religious experience, there's no other book (except for the Holy Bible, of course) I have consulted more frequently than *Meditations*. My copy's semi-legible scribblings in the margins, orange highlighter-striped sentences, double-underlined words that only Thurman could have scripted have endeared me to this classic.

Naturally, at some point, my treasured book's pages will begin yellowing, and what once nourished my spirit and steadied my soul through rough patches and seasonal droughts will, I hope, be another's guide. Such is my hope in offering *Just Living: Meditations for Engaging Our Life and Times* to readers of this book.

That the thoughts housed here will be forwarded to another's questioning heart is immensely gratifying, to be sure. But it is important to note up front that I am only in the middle of my fourth decade of life, carrying only so much practical wisdom from seeing the world and musing with God. So, it would be unwise to come to the pages of this book hoping for a repristination of Thurman. That, my friend, would be wagering on the impossible. Yet there's something of searching significance in the words of each meditation featured in this book, words traversing multiple biblical genres that engage history, theology, culture, and politics, and relate them to the myriad public issues and justice concerns of our times.

Just Living came about following Rose Berger's invitation for me to become a contributing editor for *Sojourners* magazine, writing

26 essays over the course of the early spring and mid-summer of 2019 for *Living the Word*, a lectionary-based Bible study combining biblical exegesis with social justice commentary. From February to July, by the 15th of each month, Rose expected 1,600 words on her desk, no excuses.

Before things were underway, Rose heavily stressed that I put my best thoughts forward. "We want your voice! Let Kenyatta be Kenyatta!" she urged. Frankly, at the time, I wasn't sure if I knew the Kenyatta of which she spoke since I would be neither writing a sermon, a why-to- how-to-preaching manual, nor preparing an academic paper written in dissertation-speak. But after Rose's review of batch two, I was heartened more than she could have ever known by her words of reply, which read, "I think you have the knack!" So, Rose, for your careful attention to detail and gentle coaching, I am beyond grateful.

Just Living, Volume 1, is organized into three parts. Each part consists of a themed introduction paired with a set of four to five meditations. Of special note, the biblical exposition done for each meditation could center on one or several from the set of Scripture readings assigned for the week. And, finally, concluding each meditation is a short prayer and discussion questions for further reflection.

This book is intended to be a devotional Bible study for an intergenerational, racially and ethnically diverse, politically and socially conscious lay readership for whom biblical scholarship and cultural criticism written in journalistic prose is highly valued. Whether used for daily personal meditation, journaling, facilitating Bible discussion groups, or broaching one-on-one dialogue with a religiously disaffected person, this exploration of the Bible at the intersection of contemporary culture and religious faith seeks to be a formative resource for inquisitive Christians doubly burdened by the call to speak justly and lovingly in unsettling times on a planet we all hope will survive us.

As author, I have asked what I imagine Thurman might have asked himself during his writing process: "How might I speak to the most pressing demands and concerns of my times in an uncomplicated, meaningful way?" He would say, I think, as he has once before, "Don't ask what the world needs. Ask what makes you come alive and go do it. Because what the world needs is people who have come alive."

My utmost hope in the course of your reading is that you spend time in prayer and reflection, and come alive and experience a fresh appreciation for Scripture's power to kindle the imagination, form us inwardly, and motivate us to meet our evermore pressing obligation of giving a grace-filled gospel feet in today's world.

Kenyatta R. Gilbert
Howard University School of Divinity

I
Distress the Comfortable

Certain words cause problems. When I ask first-year seminarians to take seriously the importance of using inclusive language for God and humanity, who would have thought my urging would generate such panic and skepticism? The blank stares and grimaces at the suggestion that *Father God* is grammatically on par with *Heavenly Parent* or *Mother God*, theologically, says that, yet again, the God known to them is being tampered with. Perhaps the term *inclusion* is difficult for some because it means to them that all things done in word and deed that do no intentional harm to others are at worst permissible because God's love is boundless. Equally fraught is the term *expansion*. Notions of colonialism, Manifest Destiny, and Christian triumphalism come to mind.

How did the words *inclusive* and *expansion* become such problematic, polarizing terms? One might place blame squarely on postmodernity's shoulders with its demand that Christians shed their husks of credulity and theological defensiveness. Others argue that for Christians to be taken seriously today they must join the postmodern conversation with a revelation that can hold up in a world of scientific advancement and Twitter.

In this first set of meditations, we are given tools to see how examination of the past informs the present and ushers us into the wide embrace of a loving God who sends believers out to do big things. God invites non-Israelites into wholeness; leads the faint-hearted to joy; distresses the comfortable who cooperate with evil, and reassures followers sent out as "lambs before wolves" that the promises of the sender are trustworthy.

1. Scenes and Signals
2 Kings 5:1-14; Psalm 30; Luke 10:1-11, 16-20; Galatians 6:1-16

Community wellness is a divine concern. God enters and exits the moving scenes of Scripture in unsuspecting places and in the acts of unlikely people to signal God's presence. In 2 Kings, unnamed servants act as divine emissaries who lead the powerful and mighty commander Naaman to shed his cultural arrogance, heed the wise counsel of the prophet Elisha, and confess faith in YHWH.

Unnamed actors play pivotal roles in God's liberative work. We see the divine at work in the voice of the captured Israelite servant girl of Naaman's wife (2 Kings 5:2), in the desperate appeal of Naaman's servants (2 Kings 5:13), and in the emboldened testimony of the 70 commissioned evangelists (Luke 10:1) who put demons to flight (Luke 10:17). An all-star cast of anonymous diplomats is pressed into the service of God to ensure that God's agenda for communal restoration is accomplished. For this reason, it would be unbiblical for anyone to claim that one's scriptural anonymity would necessarily equal absence of agency.

Each year, CNN recognizes culturally anonymous heroes who do life-giving work around the globe. They build wells in drought-stricken areas; they forgo vacations to repair cleft palates; they join Teach for America to aid educationally underserved communities. It is easy to focus our attention on the singular charismatic leader who rallies the troops into action when harm is done to communities of struggle. But we cannot underestimate the generosity of soup-kitchen chefs and environmental engineers who elect to do the work of community repair and maintenance behind the scenes without fanfare and fuss.

In a time rife with political chaos, it is difficult to remember that at the signal of a beneficent Creator, unrecognized angels have been dispatched to perform their holy work in the world. Unnamed lives matter. Through Scripture's unnamed actors, communal restoration comes in the form of healing leprosy, soul rescue from formidable foes (Psalm 30), gentleness and burden-bearing after transgression (Galatians 6:1-2), and victory over Satan and other principalities that block God's mission to save not only Israel, but also the entire world (Luke 10:16).

Prayer

Thank you, dear God, for using human means to perform your community-building holy work in the world. Help me to shed egocentric behaviors and recognize that your restoration agenda surpasses my need to shine. Disturb my conscience when I seek glory due you, and give me a willing spirit not to look past an opportunity to provide assistance to persons in need. Amen.

Questions for Reflection

1. How often do you respond to another's needs without hesitation? When God tugs at your heartstrings, do you stubbornly resist? If you are hesitant, can you list three reasons why eagerly responding to the needs of others is a challenge?

2. We are often supported in ways that elude our recognition of divine help. Reflect on a moment when you needed a problem addressed in which you alone could not fix it.

3. Think about a person you have helped without anyone else's knowledge of the act. What motivated you to withhold broadcasting the act?

2. World Prophet
Psalm 82; Amos 7:7-17; Luke 10:25-37

Judgment and mercy are at the heart of God in a world gone awry. The prophet Amos forecasts the death of King Jeroboam and Israel's exile to Babylon as God's punitive judgment for the king's iniquitous behavior (Amos 7:17). The doomsday oracle comes to unwelcoming recipients. No wonder the prophet refuses the designation *nabi* ("prophet") and says, "I am no prophet, nor a prophet's son; but I am a herdsman, and dresser of sycamore trees" (Amos 7:14). To which God says, Not so fast, sir! I have an assignment for you, Amos, because you alone can be trusted to report what you see in your age of mass deception. This is the expressed nature of the prophet's duty. And according to Amaziah, "the land is not able to bear all [Amos's] words" (Amos 7:10).

But what if God seems not to be attending to the evident woes in our world, and the divine response to injustice is stalled? The psalmist advises that we not lose hope. Despite what is seen, God rouses in response to our pleas for justice and is poised to do battle for the weak, the orphan, the destitute because God has taken up residence in the divine council—a residence for judging the nations of the earth (Psalm 82:1-4, 8).

Opposite judgment is *hesed* ("mercy"). In Jesus' parable, mercy is epitomized in the actions of a supposed religious heretic, a Samaritan, whom Jesus elevates to sainthood because of his behavior. Jesus teaches the lawyer in the story's front matter that loving God with heart, mind, soul, and strength "is all good" but is only the midterm exam. Going out into a world beyond the safety of one's tribe and into the heart of another of different cultural or religious stripe—that is the final exam. The two other actors in the passage, whom we are expected to believe will be mercy-givers, failed the test due to reticence or unwillingness.

Neighborliness is often found in the heart of socially disqualified people. Who knows? The social pariah next door may be our window of hope when left for dead (Luke 10).

Prayer

Merciful God, thank you for being a God who forgives and supplies me with spiritual courage to face powers and principalities that seek to do my family, community, and me harm. Help me to call to mind my daily need for forgiveness and to widen my heart to others seeking my forgiveness. Remind me of times when I have wronged others and have expected to receive their forgiveness and yours. Have mercy on me, O God, and equip me with the spiritual resources needed to take on assignments that are mine to assume and manage. In Jesus' name I pray. Amen.

Questions for Reflection

1. Do you consider yourself a "tell it like it is" person, or are you one who becomes overly anxious when having to speak the truth or a word of warning to someone whose actions are morally indefensible?

2. Call to mind a time when you felt some immoral behavior or an act of injustice was beyond forgiving. What infraction has taken place in your life or another's life you have found difficult to forgive?

3. Should mercy-giving have limits? If so, why?

3. Act for Others

Psalm 52; Amos 8:1-12

Naming our social location is a fundamental first step of truth-telling. In line with this logic, let us muse a bit more about Amos—a sheepherder, sycamore tree-dresser, and country prophet.

During the relatively peaceful reigns of King Uzziah in Judah and King Jeroboam II in Israel, Amos prophesied doom and destruction. Having this backdrop in mind is terribly important for a well-formed picture of the prophet's central concerns, which are inseparably tied to his social situation: merchants defrauding customers in the marketplace (Amos 2:6); the religiously arrogant defaming worship (Amos 2:8; 5:21-24); father and son committing morally reprehensible sexual acts (Amos 2:7); the wealthy and self-indulgent minority enjoying and parading their material excess (Amos 2:8; 6:4-7); and acts of bribery and dishonest governmental practices privileging few and disenfranchising others (Amos 5:11-12).

Then, as interpreters of Scripture, we arrive at Chapter 8 with eyes wide open to hear the rationale behind the judgment of the exasperated Sovereign, who says to the reluctant-turned-strident message-bearer: "The end has come upon my people Israel; I will never again pass them by. The songs of the temple shall become wailings in that day, . . . the dead bodies shall be many, cast out in every place" (Amos 8:2-3). Why? Because the powerful "trample on the needy and bring to ruin the poor of the land" (Amos 8:4).

When the abuse of the poor represents the spirit of the times, while the deceitful "all day long . . . are plotting destruction" for others (Psalm 52:1-2) because they "love evil more than good . . . lying more than speaking the truth" (Psalm 52:3), then what the psalmist intones as true for the ancients bears truth for those who fail to take refuge in God today. Truth be told, "God will break you down forever; [God] will snatch and tear you from your tent; [God] will uproot you from the land of the living" (Psalm 52:5-6).

Prayer

O Lord God, giver of mercy and judgment, help me to speak a relevant witness in dark times. Let me not lose hope in the face of human tragedy, but trust that you will right wrongs in our world in the end. Deliver us from fear and evil, and open our eyes to your truth and faithful love. Give me Amos's heart. Amen.

Questions for Reflection

1. Amos finds himself in a world in which his social environment is fraught with sexual immorality and societal neglect. What troubling world concerns does God want you to engage?

2. What should we contemporaries do in light of God's ancient pronouncement "The end has come"?

3. Name and discuss three things you or your church can undertake in response to the abuse of the poor.

4. Come and Pray
Luke 11:1-13

After Jesus finished praying in a certain place, one of his disciples requests spiritual guidance: "Lord, teach us to pray, as John taught his disciples" (Luke 11:1). Jesus responds by offering them Christianity's best-known invocation: The Lord's Prayer. In fact, this prayer is the only prayer that Jesus gives us. It is the model. In its words of petition, we get a glimpse of an alternative reality, what it means to participate with God in repairing the severed lines of communication between creature and Creator. Luke's Jesus, the rabbi of all rabbis, is a sage and prayer teacher who provides wisdom for finding safe haven in an unsafe world.

But the curious thing to notice about this prayer is its petitionary tone. Luke's record contains no appeals for divine favor. What we have here in Luke's record are five requests for God to act. Every petition in the Lord's Prayer is a request for nearness: Teach us to pray so we can know we are not alone in this world; give us food daily for our bodies; embrace us so we might know we have been forgiven; and let your kingdom come, let it come as near as it is out of our reach. These are all requests for real presence, except the final petition: Let no trial come our way. Do not bring us into the time of trial.

The Lord's Prayer is not some perfunctory prayer for the faint of heart. Martin Luther King Jr.'s mother was slain by a mentally deranged man while she was at her church's organ playing the Lord's Prayer set to music. If we carefully consider this prayer, we discover that persistence—asking, seeking, knocking—is rewarded with the gift of divine compassion.

God's gift of real presence is the site of God's kingdom at hand. When we pray as Luke's Jesus instructs us to pray, we find a God who meets our needs and teaches us how to give of ourselves in benevolent and gracious ways.

Prayer

Our Father in heaven, hallowed be your name. Your kingdom come, your will be done, on earth as it is in heaven. Give us this day our daily bread, and forgive us our debts, as we also have forgiven our debtors. And lead us not into temptation, but deliver us from evil. Amen.

Questions for Reflection

1. How closely do you listen to the words of the Lord's Prayer while praying it? Try praying this prayer using four different translations (e.g. NRSV, NIV, CEB, *The Message*), and note what the experience was like for you.

2. What are you petitioning God to do for you and for others?

3. Does God reward our persistence?

II

End of the White Throne

The nature of dishonor and consequence are what these passages teach. For the average Bible reader, the front matter of the Book of Hosea alone—specifically the first three chapters—disturbs the conscience. At the site of Hosea's calling, God's first words are "Go, take for yourself a wife of whoredom and have children of whoredom, for the land commits great whoredom by forsaking the Lord" (Hosea 1:2). Wow!

The writer of Hebrews proposes an alternate reality: Any reality worth seeing comes into view through faith in the unseen (Hebrews 11:1). The prophet Isaiah sees what God sees through another portrait. Like believers today, sightings of empty rituals and defiled worship strain Isaiah's eyes. When harsh judgment is meted out in Scripture, it is generally in response to an act of rebellion or for defaulting on a covenantal agreement. An ashamed and aggrieved

God enters our contemporary global vineyard, asking Christians today, "What more was there to do for my vineyard that I have not done in it? When I expected it to yield grapes, why did it yield wild grapes?" (Isaiah 5:1-3a).

The essential work of the guardian is to protect the investments. While we are not permitted to "psychologize" the prophet Jeremiah, we can still say that shame is evident. To say, "Why me, God?" rather than "Why not me?" is to be imprisoned by a faulty internal transcript.

1. Sin-Stained Garments
Psalm 107:1-9, 43; Hosea 11:1-11; Colossians 3:1-11

When perfectly landed on the ear of one nabbed for some error of judgment or misdeed, the reprimand "Shame on you" intends to trigger remorse in the perceived offender. Shame works on the psyche in ways distinguishable from guilt. Guilt addresses human behavioral defects. Shame, on the other hand, means living in the prison of a marred internal transcript. Guilt leads one to say, "Forgive me, I was wrong to hurt or offend you." By contrast, shame says self-referentially, "I am wrong, irredeemably so, and will never be good enough."

There is no build-up in Hosea. God goes straight for the jugular to shame a disloyal covenant partner; and the prophet Hosea and his wife, Gomer, are called to the stage to act things out. Husband Hosea is metaphorically cast as the deity; wife Gomer as the promiscuous Israel. One must take great care when handling such theologically problematic texts as are found in the opening chapters of Hosea, using imagery that cast a male as God and a female as sinful and unchaste.

If such texts are not understood properly, some have used them to justify violence against women. More properly, in Hosea 11, we find God cast as parent and Israel as the wayward one. "When

Israel was a child, I loved him. . . . It was I who taught Ephraim to walk, I took them up in my arms. . . . I bent down to them and fed them" (Hosea 11:1, 3, 4). And yet, "the more I called them, the more they went from me" (Hosea 11:2). God reaches toward Israel and Ephraim in tenderness, and the household of faith turns away.

In the next scene, there enters an ashamed God coming with mercy and compassion to share. "How can I give you up, Ephraim? How can I hand you over, O Israel?" (Hosea 11:8). The Northern Kingdom becomes an Assyrian vassal but eludes annihilation with six words of divine justification: "I am God and no mortal" (Hosea 11:9). This same God remains steadfast in desert-like conditions; satisfies hungry and wearied souls; orchestrates mighty acts of deliverance (Psalm 107); and demands good ethics, such as "putting on salvation" and shedding sin-stained garments for new ones as a sign of our baptism (Colossians 3).

Prayer
Satisfy my weary soul this day, dear God. Make my life brand-new; deliver me from shame; purge me from the guilt that weighs heavily on me; and help me to understand the depth of your steadfast love, salvation, and forgiveness. In Jesus' name I pray. Amen.

Questions for Reflection
1. Recall a moment from your childhood when you felt shamed. Sit quietly with that moment for four minutes, and then release it to God. Resolve not to dwell on it anymore.

2. What guilt are you carrying right now? Pray the prayer once more, and listen for God's plan on how to be freed of it during your day.

3. Disrupt the internal transcript, and commit to saying one thing good about yourself every day (e.g. I am bold. I am beautiful. I have a great smile.)

2. New Social Order
Isaiah 1:1, 10-20; Luke 12:32-40; Hebrews 11:1-3, 8-16

The letter to the Hebrews is a sermon by an anonymous Christian to a largely Gentile Jewish audience in the aftermath of the First Jewish–Roman War. This community now found their towns decimated, their land seized by Roman forces, and the Temple in Jerusalem destroyed. Pressured to reclaim a sense of religious identity, the sermon encourages those whose faith was traumatized not to shrink back from proclaiming Christ.

Chapter 11 urges the displaced and dismayed converts to remember the lives of faithful forebears who trusted God and practiced faith without the Temple. Such trust inspires doxology because what was divinely spoken to the ancestors by the prophets remains continuous in the proclamation of the promised heir, Jesus Christ. This Jesus arrives in the narrative rightly positioned in the Abrahamic procession of persons "who by faith" searched for a homeland of permeable borders, a heavenly city not walled by human means. The writer of Hebrews reminds that such trust will be rewarded by access to a God not ashamed to be called their God (Hebrews 11:16).

The prophet Isaiah does not see a bruised or broken people. His vision is occupied by the wickedness of his kinsfolk. The Lord says, "What to me is the multitude of your sacrifices? . . . I have had enough of burnt offerings. . . . When you stretch out your hands, I will hide my eyes from you; even though you make many prayers,

I will not listen" (Isaiah 1:11, 15). Do we have eyes to see what the prophet saw in our context of racial intolerance and religious bigotry?

Whether watching energy regulations abandoned to allow more drilling offshore, or hearing of real estate encroachment of lands set aside for descendants of war-decimated persons indigenous to these shores, or passively looking on as politically conservative policy wonks drive legislation to gut healthcare benefits and food programs for the economically vulnerable, Jesus asks of us the hard thing.

In Luke 12, Jesus gives a command: "Sell your possessions and give alms" (Luke 12:33). The wisdom of Jesus' words to his disciples regarding parting with the social trappings of wealth gives rise to trusting the voice speaking from the text: "Do not be afraid, little flock," for God wants to give you a new social order (Luke 12:32), an incorruptible treasure.

Prayer
Dear God, I confess that I am guilty of wanting to turn back from what you expect of me to do. My faith has been put to the test more often than not, and I often feel ashamed that I am afraid to accept the next challenging assignment ahead. Help me to refocus my concern, knowing that you are the pioneer and perfecter of faith and that there is no obstacle, test, or circumstance I can experience that you have not already fully felt. I trust that you are with me. Amen.

Questions for Reflection
1. Read Hebrews 11–12, and then ask yourself, What am I afraid of?

2. How often do you sit with your life to mark moments when God has been faithful in helping you to overcome a challenge or an obstacle? Take a moment now and describe two profound moments when this has happened.

3. Jesus often asks us to exchange something we value in order to receive some spiritual benefit. What are you being asked to give up or give away and have found it difficult to do?

3. Growth of Evil

Psalm 80:1-2, 8-19; Isaiah 5:1-7; Luke 12:49-56

In his sermon "Automatic Earth," theologian Howard Thurman insists that when barriers to growth are removed and conditions are right, then the yield from seeds planted in soil is assured. But to the people of Judah, Isaiah sings a different ditty. "My beloved had a vineyard on a very fertile hill. . . . Dug it and cleared it of stones, and planted it with choice vines; [then] built a watchtower in the midst of it . . . [and] expected it to yield grapes, but it yielded wild grapes" (Isaiah 5:1-2). In other words, God planted and expected justice, but instead saw bloodshed of the oppressed. To make the point crystal clear, the prophet repeats verse two's lyrics in verse four.

Psalm 80 marshals similar imagery. The shepherd of Israel leads the flock of the people out of Egypt and clears the ground for planting them in fertile soil (Psalm 80:1-2; 8-12). Yet an unrepentant people forsake care of God's vineyard. Neglect is the antithesis of responsible guardianship. Irresponsible stewards forsake salvation and receive hard judgment. Therefore, guardians must be alert to matters that threaten the planter's purposes.

Jesus reminds the crowds that his coming was to bring judgment, not tranquility. If they dwell on what's here today and gone tomorrow and remain spiritually clueless, then they know nothing about divine ecology, nothing about understanding God's life-giving purposes (Luke 12). To haphazard meteorologists, Jesus says, "When you see a cloud rising in the west, you immediately say, 'It is going to rain'; and so, it happens. And when you see the south wind blowing, you say, 'There will be scorching heat,' and it happens. You hypocrites!"

This throat-clearing rebuke heard by the crowd beckons Christians to confront a truth many do not intend to accept as fact. The fact that we must live in a world that supports growth, even the growth of evil and suffering born of myriad forms of spiritual hypocrisy. And if you think Jesus came to bring peace in the face of hypocrisy, Jesus says, "No, I tell you" I do justice by division.

Prayer
Dear Lord, let me be found doing your justice work in the world in these desperate and confusing times. Let me not be a spiritual hypocrite, but rather a striver working to develop a matured devotional life—one that unites compassion, truth-telling, and thoughtfulness. Amen.

Questions for Reflection
1. Do you equate suffering with evil?

2. What theological supports do you bring to the belief that good will triumph over evil in the end?

3. Are there any tangible signs that you have discerned in recent years that have impressed upon you a sense of urgency in preparing for Jesus' second coming?

4. An Inherent Dignity
Jeremiah 1:4-10

Can you imagine God saying to you in childhood, as to Jeremiah, "You will overthrow kingdoms, uproot evil, and tear down walls"? (Jeremiah 1:10). That sounds intimidating, right?

Appointed during King Josiah's reign, this seventh-century prophet receives God's commission to be a herald. Babylon has emerged as a new threat to Judah. The Northern Kingdom has been captured following the destruction of the Temple. Mass deportations of artisans, sentinels, and aristocrats are underway. And to boot, flanking Judah's southern border is the old nemesis, Egypt.

Jeremiah emerges from the womb into this charged political environment to receive his ordination papers. No one wants the work of convincing unrepentant monarchs that their tightly held belief in divine protection might be revocable. At least for Jeremiah, God says reassuringly, "Do not be afraid of them, for I am with you to deliver you" (1:8). The work to which Jeremiah is called is scandalous. The prophet will have to face the daily reminders that the social environment in which he was formed is religiously and politically poisoned.

At the heart of Jeremiah's vocation is the work of helping his kinspeople to critically examine the merits of their deeply embedded faith claims. The work of dislodging deeply embedded beliefs about racial and ethnic superiority, for example, in a society that has enthroned whiteness is far more formidable a challenge than nurturing a baby from speechlessness to adulthood to see the inherent dignity and worth of all people. How can we be saved from the sham of shame?

Jesus had no problem breaking shameful custom to heal a woman who had endured a debilitating condition for 18 years. Not unlike the spiritual fistfights into which Jeremiah would later be called, Jesus meets the religious gatekeepers who exalt protection of tradition over human life with shaming words: "You hypocrites!" Let us not earn the same label.

Prayer

Creator God, help me to respond affirmatively when you call me into particular assignments I may feel unprepared to assume. Let me rest in peaceful assurance knowing that wherever I am sent you will meet me there. Amen.

Questions for Reflection

1. Put yourself in Jeremiah's shoes for a moment. What would be your greatest concern if God spoke in a future-oriented way about what you'd be doing this time next year?

2. Read Jeremiah 1 again. Take a moment of pause, and just sit with your thoughts.

3. What concerns do you have about performing your ministry calling in this current political environment?

III

The Life-Giving Presence of a Debt-Canceling God

Wealth advisers teach us why and where to stockpile our assets and how to diminish our liabilities. "Save! Save! Save! Put away for rainy days. Establish your kid's college nest egg now! Buy low, and sell high! Get real estate to get more bang for your buck! Don't touch your 401k or risk having nothing for retirement!" And, of course, they earnestly urge, "Set aside enough for taxes, or be bitten by Uncle Sam in the end!"

Any good wealth adviser aims to cure their clients of unsound "robbing Peter to pay Paul" financial practices. Managing portfolios calls for vigilance because markets can be highly volatile and thus vulnerable to external forces beyond one's control. For this reason, sound investment strategy requires advance planning, goal-setting, and staying focused.

The Gospel readings that follow address the importance of honoring one's faith journey by carefully calculating costs and practicing disciplined stewardship. These themes color the pages of Luke's Gospel but also inform Paul's eldering counsel to his young devotee Timothy. Paul writes, "There is great gain in godliness combined with contentment" (1 Timothy 6:6), for true satisfaction is discovered at the site of contentedness, not on "the uncertainties of riches" (6:17).

Our spiritual ledgers get out of whack when wealth accrual is decoupled from gratitude and when we forsake practical wisdom. Relaxing the spiritual appetite to hoard temporal goods is not only good stewardship, but crucial for securing tomorrow's sacred dividends. Having an appropriate perspective on wealth is the initial deposit for moving into the life-giving presence of a debt-canceling God.

1. Forsaking Fidelity

Psalm 81:1, 10-16; Jeremiah 2:4-13; Hebrews 13:1-8, 15-16

Biblical storylines of God's dealings with Israel vary little in terms of plot. The master narrative of unrequited love loops over and again in the prophetic literature. Taglines proceed on this order: "As they pursued worthless things, they forgot their first love and were forced to submit to the exacting demands of their foreign foes. Yet again, a faithful God is love-spurned by a prized people who contented themselves with serving lesser gods of their own making."[1]

Sacred love tales of this sort get nauseating, to say the least—at least I think so. One would think that a people with whom God is madly in love could get it together, right? But because of our acts of spiritual infidelity, we humans exchange secured glory for things that do not profit us, forsaking living water in exchange for leaky cisterns that cannot hold water (Jeremiah 2:11, 13).

A better conclusion to a sacred love story is praying open-heartedly. "Let not, O God, my serial disregard of the provisions you supply bring insult to your love—a love so undeserved." Spiritual infidelity causes believers to leave the finest wheat in the field and forsake the satisfaction of tasting sweet honey from the rock (Psalm 81:16). Fidelity in faith is remembering that angels often masquerade as strangers and that following Jesus binds us to the locked-up and politically locked-out ones (Hebrews 13:2, 3) legally subjected to voter disenfranchisement, employment discrimination, and jury-service exclusion in America's unforgiving debtors' prisons.

Prayer

Loving and kind God, let not my serial disregard of the provisions you supply bring insult to your love, a love so undeserved. Show me how to remain disciplined in my daily walk with you. And when I forget your faithfulness, unsettle my confidence, and gently point me in the right direction. Amen.

Questions for Reflection

1. Has there ever been a moment when you said, "What I did must have really hurt God's heart." How did you manage the situation?

2. In your judgment, are churches safe spaces to process personal regret?

3. How does spiritual fidelity and justice concern inform one another? Must they go hand in hand?

2. Spoiled and Reworked
Psalm 139:1-6, 13-18; Jeremiah 18:1-11

Except for a session of good rugged outdoor play, nothing brings Ava, my nine-year-old, greater joy after a stressful school day than flattening and twisting Play-Doh or pulling apart "kid slime," which she creates from Elmer's glue, glitter, and borax. Correct apportionment of these ingredients at the molder's table is critical for prolonging shelf life and getting things rightly textured. Though inevitable messes come with the task, Ava takes full responsibility for what she creates and is unwilling to abandon the process until the slime's consistency suits her purposes.

Reach back to the wisdom Jeremiah shares, and gain similar perspective about humanity's need for God-initiated mercy and reformation. Join Jeremiah at the potter's wheel, where communal repentance stays the potter's hands, though destroying the clay was on the agenda. Gospel singer Tramaine Hawkins lyricized so well in her chart-topping song "The Potter's House" when speaking of (or singing about) a God who repairs shattered dreams and mends spiritual brokenness, who puts our lives back together.

Making frequent trips to the potter's house and seeing the potter at work meticulously twisting and flattening, restoring and refashioning life marred by sin would do us some good. Correspondingly, the psalmist remixes this sentiment of holy intimacy and sets it to song, "O LORD, you have searched me and known me. . . . For it was you who formed my inward parts; you knit me together in my mother's womb. I praise you, for I am fearfully and wonderfully made" (Psalm 139:1, 13-14a).

Prayer

O Lord, you have searched me and known me intimately. In fact, you are closer to me than my conscious awareness of myself. To be known in this way is tremendously comforting to my soul. So, I thank you. I thank you for the many character-defining moments that have conspired to bring me closer to you. And I rejoice knowing that the tests and challenges that have arisen in my life have been met by your desire to transform them for your good purposes and my good. Help me to remain moldable and useful in my service to you and humankind. Amen.

Questions for Reflection

1. What is your definition of *spiritual intimacy*?

2. Are there other images in Scripture—other than the potter's wheel—that speak in similar ways about God's intimate ways with God's people?

3. Whose life are you shaping, and why is your investment in that person's life important to you?

4. Lost and Recovered
Luke 15:1-10

In Luke 15, Jesus shares three parables. Each depicts something different about the reign of God. Three sets of circumstances, three distinctive responses, each symbolic of the human condition and how God responds to it. Each describes humanity's great debt, and each collapses into an illusion to Christ's great payment. If these parables reveal nothing else, they at the very least show us that one does not get to joy without sacrifice. Salvation is for personal and social transformation. We humans repeatedly need deliverance from sin because it impairs our ability to fulfill our God-given covenantal obligations.

Despite the multiple meanings of the concept of salvation, according to theologian Frederick Ware, Christians commonly hold to three notions about salvation. While quarreling happens over "how," the first commonly held affirmation is that Christ saves. A second affirmation is that divine action cannot be substituted or superseded by human action, which is to say that no matter how complemented by human endeavor, salvation does not happen without God's activity or without God acting first. And, third, salvation always implies that some transformation happens, whether this means improvement of one's life station; freedom from spiritual malady; or, in the case of sheep, rejoining the fold, or being found, like the unnamed woman's recovered silver drachma after being negligently handled.[2]

Salvation merits celebration. "Just so, I tell you, there is joy in the presence of the angels of God over one sinner who repents" (Luke 15:10).

Prayer

Gracious God, thank you for the manifold ways in which you have made known your will to save. I give thanks for your presence in my heart and the evidences of your activity for the collective good of our society and the world. I acknowledge today that it is not your desire that anyone finds themselves lost—whether by means of some spiritual crisis, sin entanglement, or act of hubris. But yours is the desire to save and celebrate our homecomings. I ask that you would draw lost lives to your welcoming love this day, and teach me to abide in the freedom of and hope for my salvation. Let my life be continually renewed and changed. Amen.

Questions for Reflection

1. What does it mean to be saved?

2. How was *salvation* defined for you when coming to faith?

3. In what ways can we reimagine what salvation means? Is salvation merely preparation for the afterlife? What difference does salvation make in the here-and-now?

4. The Poverty of Wealth

Luke 16:1-13

Psychologist Mardy Grothe coined the term *oxymoronica*, which he defines as tantalizing, "self-contradictory statements or observations that on the surface appear false or illogical, but at a deeper level are profoundly true."[3] For instance, Jean-Paul Sartre's statement "Human life begins on the far side of despair"[4] or Gloria Steinem's quip "I hate intolerant people" or the Confucian aphorism "Real knowledge is to know the extent of one's own ignorance" are each emblematic of the term.

As Luke 16 puts it, self-preservation directs the hired hand to bargain to make a cheater's system more honest. Can we blame the alleged dishonorable manager, under indictment for squandering his master's wealth, in an exploitative system? Has he not run out of options? Desperate times call for quick thinking and a dose of shrewdness.

One-time debt forgiveness in a corrupt payday loan system, for example, constitutes a temporary fix. When systems are rigged, many people will soon find themselves indebted again if self-same social policies persist; they will repeatedly find themselves at the mercy of the manager who will not relent. Clearing ledgers of poor people without providing job training, wealth-building options, and educational opportunity ensures more poverty.

Freedom until the next crop fails or next subsidy is needed is no security. Acting shrewdly to beat a system that devalues honest brokering cannot be a system trusted to be just in the end. The best security for children of light, Luke's Jesus oxymoronically suggests, is to make friends by means of dishonest wealth to find welcome into "the eternal homes" (Luke 16:9).

Prayer

Dear God, make me more honest with myself and continuously in search of your will for my life. Help me to be a good steward over all things entrusted to my care. I want to please you in all areas of my life. Guide me in my quest to be more disciplined in mind and spirit. Amen.

Questions for Reflection

1. How would you distinguish providing social services from doing social justice?

2. Can you blame the dishonest steward for acting shrewdly? Is there room for this sort of behavior in the Christian walk?

3. Share some of your thoughts about debt-making and debt elimination?

5. Storing Up Contentment
Luke 16:19-31; 1 Timothy 6:6-19

Englishman Lord Achton's popular dictum, "Power tends to corrupt, and absolute power corrupts absolutely" parallels in sentiment with Paul's wise counsel to his protégé Timothy: Beware Timothy, Paul fervently advises, loving money is a snare and becomes the source of all manner of evil (1 Timothy 6:10). Differently put, greedy power has no end.

To Achton's credit, his knack for naming reality in the context of empire is remarkable for one whose pedigree came from a colonizing race of people. Achton writes, "There is not a more perilous or immoral habit of mind than the sanctifying of success."[5]

The rich man dressed in purple garb who dined sumptuously everyday, signifying his immense wealth and extravagant taste, condemns himself to perpetual torment in the afterlife because he put purse before principle. Conversely, Lazarus, the poor man who had suffered greatly in his earthly life finds consolation, contentment, and surcease after dying. In death, the rich man is judged harshly not because he had acquired immense wealth. Rather, he deservingly, as the parable illustrates, is banished to Hades—the place of eternal torment—because he lacked compassion, trivialized the plight of the suffering poor, and ignored mercy extended to him while living (Luke 16:19-25).

Adding "godliness" (*eusebeia*) or "religion" combined with "contentment" (1 Timothy 6:6-7) to one's spiritual portfolio is a reminder for us to see that we brought nothing into this world and can take nothing to the grave with us.

Prayer

Dear Lord, thank you for good gifts great and small. Help me to keep your material blessings in proper perspective and to be a worthy steward of what I receive. Many are hungry, and world poverty is lamentable and preventable. Open wide hearts to share of their bounty, and let me not make my wealth my grave. Let my life be an offering. I want to die emptied of all things that would frustrate or disrupt a holy encounter with you.

Questions for Reflection

1. In our money-making, consumer-driven culture, what hopeful signs, if any, do you see that communicate that all of life does not center on material gain?

2. Describe your historical relationship with money in three short sentences.

3. Can one be simultaneously godly and exceedingly wealthy? If not, why? If so, how?

Notes

[1] The Life-giving Presence of a Debt-cancelling God," by Kenyatta Gilbert, *Sojourners Magazine*, September/October 2019 (https://tinyurl.com/yfy7mx3x).

[2] *African American Theology: An Introduction*, by Frederick L. Ware (Westminster John Knox Press, 2016); pages 153-154.

[3] *Oxymoronica: Paradoxical Wit and Wisdom From History's Greatest Wordsmiths*, by Mardy Grothe (Harper Paperbacks, 2015).

[4] *Les Mouches* [*The Flies*], by Jean-Paul Sartre (1943).

[5] *Lectures on Modern History*, by John Emerich Edward Dalberg, Lord Acton (Macmillan and Company, 1906).

www.ingramcontent.com/pod-product-compliance
Lightning Source LLC
Chambersburg PA
CBHW042035120726
47911CB00027B/746